my itty-bitty bio

Crazy Horse

Published in the United States of America by Cherry Lake Publishing Group
Ann Arbor, Michigan
www.cherrylakepublishing.com

Reading Adviser: Beth Walker Gambro, MS, Ed., Reading Consultant, Yorkville, IL
Book Designer: Jennifer Wahi
Illustrator: Jeff Bane

Photo Credits: © Holly Kuchera/Shuttershock, 5; © Aksinia Prokhorova/Shuttershock, 7; © Public Domain/Library of Congress/LOC No. 92522110, 9; © Public Domain/Library of Congress/LOC No. 2005694875. 11; © Public Domain/NPGallery/NPS No. LIBI_00312_10951, 13; © Public Domain/Library of Congress/LOC No. 96515425, 15, 22; © Library of Congress/Painted by Charles M. Russell/LOC No. 99472670, 17, 23; © Public Domain/Library of Congress/LOC No. 97505606, 19; © Igor Golovniov/Shuttershock, 21; Cover, 1, 6, 16, 18, Jeff Bane; Various frames throughout, © Shutterstock Images

Copyright © 2023 by Cherry Lake Publishing Group
All rights reserved. No part of this book may be reproduced or utilized in any form or by any means without written permission from the publisher.

Cherry Lake Press is an imprint of Cherry Lake Publishing Group.

Library of Congress Cataloging-in-Publication Data

Names: Thiele, June, author. | Bane, Jeff, 1957- illustrator.
Title: Crazy Horse / by June Thiele ; illustrator, Jeff Bane.
Description: Ann Arbor, Michigan : Cherry Lake Publishing, [2023] | Series: My itty-bitty bio
Identifiers: LCCN 2022009893 | ISBN 9781668908921 (hardcover) | ISBN 9781668910528 (paperback) | ISBN 9781668913703 (pdf) | ISBN 9781668912119 (ebook)
Subjects: LCSH: Crazy Horse, approximately 1842-1877--Juvenile literature. | Oglala Indians--Kings and rulers--Biography--Juvenile literature. | Oglala Indians--History--Juvenile literature. | Indians of North America--Great Plains--Wars--Juvenile literature.
Classification: LCC E99.O3 T54 2023 | DDC 978.004/9752440092 [B]--dc23/eng/20220314
LC record available at https://lccn.loc.gov/2022009893

Printed in the United States of America
Corporate Graphics

table of contents

My Story 4

Timeline 22

Glossary 24

Index 24

About the author: June Thiele writes and acts in Chicago where they live with their wife and child. June is Dena'ina Athabascan and Yup'ik, Indigenous cultures of Alaska. They try to get back home to Alaska as much as possible.

About the illustrator: Jeff Bane and his two business partners own a studio along the American River in Folsom, California, home of the 1849 Gold Rush. When Jeff's not sketching or illustrating for clients, he's either swimming or kayaking in the river to relax.

my story

I was born in the 1840s in South Dakota. I was part of the **Lakota tribe**. This tribe is **Native American**.

I had curly hair when I was young. My mom nicknamed me "Curly."

What are your nicknames?

Our tribe lived on a lot of land. We took care of the land. It was our home.

How do you care for your home?

But **colonizers** wanted to take our land. I fought back for my people. I was brave. My father gave me his name because of this. My name became "Crazy Horse."

I wanted the colonizers to leave us alone. I fought many wars to keep them away.

I became the war **chief** of my tribe. I protected our way of life. I protected our traditions.

I joined forces with Sitting Bull.
He was a great warrior.
We fought together. We won an important battle. It was against the U.S. Army.

But the U.S. Army **attacked** again. There were too many soldiers. We didn't have enough people fighting. We had to **surrender**.

I was killed in 1877 for fighting for my people. But my **legacy** lives on. I remind my people that they are strong.

What would you like to ask me?

timeline

1868

1840

Born 1840s

Died 1877

1876

1940

glossary

attacked (uh-TAKT) used violence against someone or something

chief (CHEEF) a leader of a tribal community or a clan

colonizers (KAH-luh-nye-zuhrz) nations or states that take control of a people or area

Lakota (luh-KOH-tuh) a Native American tribe located in South Dakota; subculture of the Sioux people

legacy (LEH-guh-see) something handed down from one generation to another

Native American (NAY-tiv uh-MER-uh-kuhn) one of the people who originally lived in America, or a relative of these people

surrender (suh-REN-duhr) to give up

tribe (TRYB) a group of people including many families, clans, or generations

index

colonizers, 10, 12
curly, 6
Sitting Bull, 16
soldiers, 18
South Dakota, 4
tribe, 4, 8, 14
U.S. Army, 16, 18
wars, 12, 14